For my son Josh, who builds with words
—F.W.W.

For those who build things to last
—T.L.

10 9 8 7 6 5 4 3 2 1

The text of this book is set in 14 pt. Leawood Book.
The illustrations are rendered in watercolors.

Library of Congress Cataloging-in-Publication Data
Weller, Frances Ward. Matthew Wheelock's wall / by Frances
Ward Weller ; illustrated by Ted Lewin. — 1st
ed.   p.   cm. Summary: Matthew Wheelock builds a stone
wall around his New England fields, and it becomes a symbol
for generations of his family. ISBN 0-02-792612-5 1. Wheelock,
Matthew—Juvenile fiction. [1. Wheelock, Matthew—Fiction. 2.
Walls—Fiction. 3. New England—Fiction.] I. Lewin, Ted, ill. II.
Title. PZ7.W454Mat 1992   [E]—dc20   91-9608

MATTHEW WHEELOCK'S WALL

by FRANCES WARD WELLER

illustrated by TED LEWIN

MACMILLAN PUBLISHING COMPANY • *NEW YORK*

Maxwell Macmillan Canada • *Toronto*

Maxwell Macmillan International • *New York*   *Oxford*   *Singapore*   *Sydney*

Old Matthew Wheelock built this wall.

A hundred years ago and more, he laid the stony necklace round his fields, from road to river.

The pastureland he needed for his crops was thick with rocks.
To plow and plant he had to clear them all away.
Beside each field he dug a shallow trench to hold great stones
he pried and towed behind his horse.

The rest piled up in hasty jumbles as he dug them out and plowed and sowed.

When all his seed was planted, Matthew went back to his piles of rocks.

Impatiently he stacked a few at random, stone on stone.

But then the art of it reached out and caught him.

He'd build to last a hundred years, a magic weaving, stone holding stone without a trace of mortar.

He turned his stones, did Matthew, studied them until he knew one from another, like his sheep.

The wall became for him a giant puzzle.

He sorted stones until his strong back ached; his callused hands were torn.

Round stones and flat, rough stones and smooth, big stones and small, went tumbling through his dreams.

Then, out at sunup, Matthew worked his puzzle. He set stones slanting inward, and used smaller ones to fill the chinks between the big.

Where two stones met, he laid another one above.
And every stone he set to touch its neighbors.

So his wall grew by day, from patterns drawn in Matthew's mind, stone hugging stone.

And while he dreamed, field mice explored by night in search of cozy crevices for nests.

The large flat stones he'd saved to cap the wall.
And even as he set them and moved on, the field mice tucked
their babies in its nooks.

At last the wall was strung round all his land.

He walked its winding length, and jumped upon a capstone now and then.

"This wall will hold!" he hollered to the sky.

He gazed across his greening fields, from road to river.

"This wall will outlast me. This wall's my monument!" he said.

That night he slept a dreamless, stoneless sleep.

Where Matthew cleared the rocks, his corn grew tall.
As summers passed his children dueled like knights and pirates on the wall.

Year in and out, his sons and grandsons worked the Wheelock fields.

And Matthew's wall was equal to the years.

Just once, when lightning felled a giant oak, the wall was breached, and mossy stones lay tumbled till Matthew's great-grandsons set them right.

It's always been a friendly sort of wall. It's home to wary chipmunks, darting snakes, and all the tribes of field mice whose ancestors crept in first.

"But I don't bother them," Jerusha Wheelock says, "and they don't bother me."

This wall's her spaceship, stage and queenly tower.
She leaps along the capstones, and she bounces now and then.
"My Great-Great-Grandpa Matthew Wheelock built this wall!"
she cries, running from road to river.

Old Matthew Wheelock was a wizard with a wall.

His need became a dream and then a plan.

And so his wall has stood more than a hundred years, stone hugging stone.

He knew the small ones need the big, the big the small.

So like the world is Matthew Wheelock's wall.